Werewolves Don't Run for President ·

Check out all the books about
The
BAILEY SCHOOL KIDS

ISBN-13: 978-0-439-65036-6
ISBN-10: 0-439-65036-4

Text copyright © 2004 by Marcia Thornton Jones and Debra S. Dadey.
Illustrations copyright © 2004 by Scholastic Inc.
All rights reserved. Published by Scholastic Inc. SCHOLASTIC, APPLE PAPERBACKS, THE ADVENTIURES OF THE BAILEY SCHOOL KIDS, and associated logos are trademarks and/or registered trademarks of Scholastic Inc.

15 14 13 12 11 10 9 8 7   8 9 10 11 12 13/0

Printed in the U.S.A.   40

This edition first printing, July 2008

Werewolves Don't Run for President

by **Debbie Dadey**
and
Marcia Thornton Jones

illustrated by John Steven Gurney

Scholastic Inc.

New York Toronto London Auckland Sydney
Mexico City New Delhi Hong Kong Buenos Aires

To Mara Rockliff — who has my vote
for being a great writing friend!
— MTJ

To Nathan Dadey — I am so proud of you.
Good luck in college!
— DD

Contents

Contents

1

President Deadly

"This is the most exciting thing to ever happen in Bailey City," Liza squealed to her good friends Eddie, Melody, and Howie. It was after school and they stood under the big oak tree on the school playground.

Eddie rolled his eyes. "Boring, just like this town."

"How can you say that?" Howie asked Eddie. "This is history in the making."

Eddie nodded. "My point exactly. History is boring and so is Bailey City. I still can't believe Mrs. Jeepers is making us go to this thing."

Melody waved her tiny American flag in Eddie's face. "If you don't go," she said, "you'll be the only third grader who doesn't get to see the person who may be the next president of the United States."

"Not only that," Howie added, "you won't be able to write your report about his speech."

"And Mrs. Jeepers will give you an F," Melody added.

Eddie groaned. "Who cares about speeches?"

"You should," Liza said. "Free speech is one of our rights!"

"Then I should be able to talk in class whenever I want," Eddie grumbled. He wasn't happy, but Eddie followed his friends to Bailey City Park where one of the candidates for president was supposed to speak. Main Street was blocked off, so the kids took a detour through the cemetery.

"I think it's so cool that Mr. Youngblood stopped here on his way to Sheldon City for the big debate," Liza told her friends. "The other party's candidate didn't even mention Bailey City."

"Party?" Eddie interrupted. "Where's the party? That sounds like more fun than going to a speech."

"Weren't you listening in class?" Melody asked.

"Of course not," Eddie said matter-of-factly.

Liza sighed. "A political party is a group that has common ideas and works to get a candidate elected," she explained.

Eddie kicked at a clod of dirt. "Why would they call something like that a party?" he grumbled.

"Who are you going to vote for in our class election?" Melody asked her friends.

The kids at Bailey School were learning about all the candidates and planned to hold a pretend election.

Howie shook his head. "That's private."

"I don't mind telling," Liza said. "I'm voting for Mr. Youngblood. What about you, Eddie?"

"Who cares? A dead guy would be more exciting for president than most politicians," Eddie said, kicking at the weeds growing beside a tombstone.

Melody carefully walked around the grave markers and told her friends, "I think I'm voting for Mr. Youngblood, too. My aunt said he's the best candidate."

"Look at me," Eddie said, popping his head up over the top of a tombstone. "I'm President Deadly. I'll never raise taxes or the dead. You can count my bones and you can count on me."

"Eddie," Liza giggled, "you are so silly."

"Politics is serious," Howie said.

"Not as serious as that!" Melody said, pointing.

2

Security

"What are you kids doing?" asked a man with a black suit and dark sunglasses. Two other men stood beside him with their hands touching tiny speakers in their ears.

"What are YOU doing?" Eddie asked.

"Eddie," Melody said, pulling Eddie away from the tombstone. "Don't be a smart aleck."

Eddie shook his head. "I'm not doing anything wrong, and the last time I checked, this was a free cemetery."

The three men flashed badges and the one wearing sunglasses explained, "We're security. We have to make sure no dangerous characters get near Mr. Youngblood."

"Oh, we're not dangerous," Liza explained. "We're going to hear the speech so we can write a report for our teacher."

The head man took off his sunglasses and leaned close to the kids. "A report, you say?" he asked in a raspy voice. "For school?"

Liza took a step back and nodded. "Our teacher assigned it."

"Work, work, work," Eddie muttered. "That's all our teacher thinks about."

"She said we had to learn about the government," Melody explained. "The more we know, the easier it will be to make a decision in our school's election."

"The fact that Bailey City is a stop on the campaign trail is a historic event," Howie added. "We've never met a presidential candidate before."

"Exactly where is this path the candidates use as a trail?" Eddie asked.

Melody rolled her eyes. "You really don't listen to Mrs. Jeepers, do you?" she said. "The campaign trail isn't a real path. It's just a way to describe places a candidate goes to make speeches and get support."

Eddie kicked a tree root. "If you ask me, a hike in the woods sounds like more fun than a campaign trail."

"Mr. Youngblood will like this," the security man told the other guards. "It fits with his platform."

The other security agents nodded.

"Follow us," the head man said.

"I don't think we should go," Liza whispered to her friends.

"We have no choice," Howie told her as the men surrounded them.

Liza gulped and squeezed Melody's hand. "Maybe we should run away," Liza said.

"I'm not going anywhere," Eddie said, planting his feet firmly on the ground and crossing his arms over his chest, "until someone tells me where you are taking us, and exactly what a school report has to do with a platform."

"Honestly," Howie said. "You are going

to fail third grade if you don't pay attention. A platform describes what a candidate believes in."

"This way," the head security agent said as he slipped his sunglasses back on. "I'm taking you to meet the next president of the United States of America!"

"Awesome!" Howie said. "That will help us get great grades on our reports."

Eddie rolled his eyes. "Or we'll be bored to death."

"This way, please," the head man said.

The three men led the kids through the cemetery and up to a group of adults gathered in the center of Bailey City Park. Banners and posters covered every tree, and a band played loud marching music.

"That's him! That's Mr. Youngblood!" Melody said, pointing at a man in a navy suit with his back to them. "Just think! He might be our next president."

"Maybe we could put in a good word

for more summer vacation," Eddie said, perking up at the thought.

The man beside Mr. Youngblood wore torn blue jeans and a stained T-shirt. "That's Mr. Jenkins, from Camp Lone Wolf," Howie whispered. "What's he doing here?"

The kids all recognized the camp counselor. His hair was pulled back in a long ponytail and the sun glistened off his dog tags. He looked like he hadn't shaved in months.

"You'd think he would have dressed up to meet the president," Liza said.

"Possible president," Howie corrected. "He has to be elected first."

Another hairy man in a flowered shirt came up to Mr. Youngblood and shook his hand. "That's Harry Goto," Melody said. "It's really strange that they're both here together." Harry Goto was a dancer the kids had seen perform at Camp Lone Wolf. The four kids had thought that both Harry and Mr. Jenkins were werewolves.

"What's so strange?" Eddie asked. "They're werewolves. They travel in packs."

"I can't believe we actually thought they were werewolves," Melody said with a giggle. "After all, there are no such things as werewolves." In broad daylight, the two men were hairy, but not too scary.

But when Mr. Youngblood turned to face the kids, Liza let out a scream that scared away birds in a nearby tree. "It's a werewolf convention!" she shrieked.

3

Werewolf for President

The presidential candidate was taller than both Mr. Jenkins and Mr. Goto by at least a foot. Mr. Youngblood's red and gray hair curled around his ears and disappeared down the collar of his suit jacket. A thick gray beard covered most of his face so that the first thing the kids noticed when they looked at him were his brown eyes — glaring.

A security agent took a step toward the four kids, and reached inside her navy blue blazer. Her eyes squinted in a frown as she talked into the microphone clipped to her collar.

Mr. Jenkins and Mr. Goto didn't seem too concerned. As soon as they saw the four kids they both howled with laughter.

Eddie grabbed Liza's elbow and pulled her behind a tree, away from the approaching security agent. Melody and Howie waved at Mr. Youngblood before ducking behind the same tree.

"How embarrassing," Melody told Liza. "You just called the next president of the United States a werewolf!"

"Maybe not," Howie corrected her. "Mr. Youngblood might not win the election."

Liza looked ready to cry. "I'm sorry," she said. "But when he turned around he was so hairy all I could think of was a giant werewolf hunting for an afternoon snack!"

"He does have a lot of reddish hair," Howie admitted as he patted Liza on the shoulder. "I can see why you were scared."

"Hey," Eddie sputtered, pulling off his ball cap and pointing to his head. "There's absolutely nothing wrong with having red hair!"

Melody shook her head. "I've heard that red-headed people can be a real handful," she said. "They act without thinking and get mad in a hurry." Eddie glared at Melody, and his fingers curled into a fist.

Howie stepped between Melody and Eddie. "Eddie *is* right. You can't judge people based on how they look," Howie said. "Just because Mr. Youngblood has more red hair than a grizzly bear doesn't mean he's a werewolf."

"But he was standing right next to two well-known wolfmen," Liza said. Her face had grown pale and her bottom lip trembled.

"We never actually proved that Mr. Jenkins and Harry Goto were wolfmen," Melody reminded her.

Liza looked really worried. "But what if they are? And what if Mr. Youngblood is a werewolf, too? What would happen to this country if a werewolf was elected president?"

Eddie shrugged. "It probably wouldn't

be so bad. My dad says a bunch of nuts have been running this country for a long time."

"You're jumping to conclusions," Melody said. "Besides, we have nothing to worry about right now. A majority of the people of the United States would have to vote for Mr. Youngblood before he could become president."

"That's right," Eddie said. "Nobody is going to elect a guy with a long, hairy beard."

Howie shook his head. "Actually, there have been lots of presidents with beards." Then he started counting off names with his fingers. "Abraham Lincoln, Ulysses Grant, Benjamin Harrison . . ."

"How do you *know* all this stuff?" Eddie asked, grabbing Howie's fingers.

"Research," Howie said matter-of-factly. "You should try it sometime."

"You could start by finding out if

werewolves have ever lived in the White House," Liza said with a whimper.

Howie shook his head again. "I'm pretty sure that werewolves don't run for president," he told her.

"I hope you're right," Liza said, peering around the tree. "Because here comes Mr. Youngblood now!"

4

Werewolf Attack

Mr. Youngblood stalked across Bailey City Park, followed by a pack of security agents. Mr. Jenkins and Harry Goto trailed behind them.

Liza whimpered, and Melody hid behind Eddie. Howie didn't budge. "May I shake your hand?" Howie asked when Mr. Youngblood stopped by their tree. "This will be great in my report!"

Mr. Youngblood scratched behind his left ear before he reached out to shake Howie's hand. Mr. Youngblood shook so hard that Howie had to grab the tree to keep from falling over.

"Your report is exactly why I sniffed you and your friends out," Mr. Youngblood said. His voice was as low and growly as a Doberman pinscher's. "I want to know

21

everything about your homework assignment," he added.

"That's the last thing I want to talk
about," Eddie told him. "Why don't you
tell us about riding in limousines, in-
stead? If you get elected president, will
you take us for a ride in *Air Force One*?"

One of the security agents stepped
toward Eddie. "Mr. Youngblood is a very

busy man," she said. "He has no time to waste on nonsense."

Mr. Youngblood held out his hand to stop the agent from continuing. Liza couldn't help but notice that thick hair peeped out from Mr. Youngblood's shirt-sleeve and curled around his knuckles.

"Limousines and airplanes are interesting," Mr. Youngblood said. "Do you really want to ride in them?"

For the first time that afternoon Eddie's grin reached from one ear to the other. "I'm ready whenever you are!" Eddie told him.

Mr. Youngblood laughed. "I *am* ready," he said. "But I think you need to do a little research first."

"Aw," Eddie said, kicking at the base of the tree with his sneakers. "You sound just like Mrs. Jeepers."

"And who might that be?" Mr. Youngblood asked.

"Mrs. Jeepers is our teacher," Liza answered politely.

"She wants us to write a report about your campaign speech," Melody said.

"We're supposed to include everything you plan to do to make our country better," Howie said. "Then we have to decide if we agree with you or not. We're going to hold our own school election to see if kids would vote the same as adults."

Mr. Youngblood listened very closely. When Howie finished explaining the assignment, the presidential candidate clapped his giant hands together.

"I'll tell you exactly what the number one item on my platform is," Mr. Youngblood told them. "Education! I plan to put education first when I'm president."

"That's one strike against you," Eddie muttered. Education was the last thing on Eddie's list.

Mr. Youngblood cocked his head, but ignored Eddie. "Tell me more about this teacher of yours," he said.

Liza looked at Melody. Melody looked

at Howie. Howie looked at his sneakers. They didn't know what to say. It was a known fact that most kids at Bailey Elementary School believed their third-grade teacher was a vampire. Eddie, however, didn't have a problem speaking up.

"Mrs. Jeepers is a monster!" Eddie blurted out. "She stays up nights just thinking of stuff for us to do. First she makes us add numbers. Then she tells us to subtract them. The next thing you know, she wants us to multiply them. Then she turns around and has us divide them. It's like she can't make up her mind. And that's just in math! You should see what she makes us do in science! I don't even want to talk about this social studies project on democracy and the presidents. It's as if she thinks we're actually going to *use* this stuff someday. *Sheesh!* Just talking about it makes my blood boil."

"A teacher that gets kids' blood boiling!" Mr. Youngblood said. "I *have* to meet this wonderful teacher of yours." Mr. Youngblood turned to the nearest security agent. "Get the principal on the phone," he barked. "Ask for an appointment first thing tomorrow morning."

"Yes, sir. Right away, sir," the agent said.

"Anyone who thinks a teacher — especially Mrs. Jeepers — is wonderful must have a brain the size of a flea," Eddie sputtered to himself.

Howie stared at the presidential candidate. "I can't believe you want to come to our school!"

"Me neither," Melody said with a grin. "Do you think this will get us A's on our papers?"

Liza didn't smile. In fact, it looked like she might cry. "You don't really want to come to our school," she told Mr. Youngblood. "There's nothing special about it at all."

"Nonsense," Mr. Youngblood said. "I bet it's a great school."

Liza shook her head. "Really, it isn't. In fact, it's so terrible that rats run wild in the hallways!"

"RATS?" Mr. Youngblood howled. He turned to yell after the agent. "Don't ask for an appointment. Demand one!"

Then Mr. Youngblood hurried away, leaving Howie, Melody, Liza, and Eddie staring at the group of people following him.

"Why in the world did you say there were rats at our school?" Melody asked.

Liza sighed. "I shouldn't have told a fib, but I was trying to save our school from a werewolf attack."

"Don't be upset," Melody said with a grin. "You didn't really lie."

"I didn't?" Liza asked.

"Of course not," Melody told her. "There is at least one giant rat running loose in the hallways of Bailey Elementary. His name is Eddie."

"Very funny, mouse brains," Eddie said.

"But I have bad news for both of you. Rats won't keep werewolves away. Werewolves nibble rats for snacks."

"Yeah," Howie said, suddenly serious. "Right before they eat kids for lunch."

5

Kids for Lunch

"I can't believe Mrs. Jeepers loves him!" Liza said as she stared at their teacher. "She even invited him to lunch!"

"I can believe it," Eddie told her. "Monsters love company."

It was the next day, and Mr. Youngblood had been true to his promise. He had come to visit Bailey Elementary and was sitting with Mrs. Jeepers at the teachers' table in the middle of the school cafeteria. In fact, almost every teacher at Bailey Elementary had squeezed in beside Principal Davis. They all wanted to meet Mr. Youngblood.

Howie shook his head. "I can't believe the next president of the United States is eating tuna noodle casserole in our cafeteria. I wish I had brought my camera."

"Remember, there's another candidate running for president. He might beat Mr. Youngblood," Liza said hopefully.

"Don't worry, there are plenty of people taking pictures," Melody said. Sure enough, one whole side of the cafeteria was filled with reporters and photographers. Outside the building, people were shouting and carrying signs as they marched in front of the school.

"What is wrong with those people?" Melody asked. "Don't they know Mr. Youngblood is a very important person? They should be more respectful."

Eddie flipped a pea across the table. "I agree," he said. "If I acted like them I'd get sent to the principal's office. Maybe they should all have to stand in a corner down at the courthouse."

Liza shook a finger at Eddie. "Don't you know anything about our Bill of Rights?" she asked.

"Who is Bill?" Eddie asked. "I don't know any Bill Wright. Is he the new kid in the fourth grade?"

Liza rolled her eyes. "Were you sleeping during class last week? The Bill of Rights isn't a person. It's a document that outlines all our rights as United States citizens, like our freedom of speech. Those demonstrators have the right to say how they feel."

"If that's the case," Eddie said, "then I think we should all make signs and march around the cafeteria demanding pizza and hot dogs every day of the week!"

"That would never work," Howie said. "Our parents wouldn't approve and we'd get in trouble."

A cameraman circled the cafeteria, shooting video of kids slurping up noodles. Melody sat up and straightened one of her black pigtails. "Everybody behave. We might be on WMTJ's six o'clock news report," she said.

Eddie flashed a smile at the cameras before complaining. "What's all the fuss about? Those people outside are giving me a headache."

"I can't believe you're complaining about noise," Liza said. "Usually you're the one making the most racket."

Eddie shrugged and blew bubbles into his chocolate milk with his straw. He kept blowing until bubbles popped out of his nose. "That'll give them something to take a picture of," he said with a laugh before wiping the chocolate boogers onto his sleeve.

"Eddie, that's gross," Melody said.

Howie ignored his friends and looked out the window. "Hey, isn't that Ranger Lily?" He knew Ranger Lily from field trips to nearby parks.

The kids crowded around a window. Hundreds of people were on the school playground carrying signs and yelling about saving the environment. Ranger Lily was one of them. "Maybe we should

tell Ranger Lily that we think Mr. Youngblood is a werewolf," Liza said.

Melody shook her head. "She wouldn't believe you. Even I don't believe you."

Liza put her hands on her hips and said, "Then I'll just have to get proof."

6

Werewolf Hunting

"I can't believe we're doing this," Melody said, turning on her flashlight. The kids had sneaked out of their houses after supper and had met back at the cemetery.

"You wanted proof that Mr. Youngblood is a werewolf," Liza told her friends, "so we're going to get proof."

Eddie leaned his head back and howled like a wolf. Dogs all over Bailey City barked in response. "What did you do that for?" Howie asked.

Eddie shrugged. "I was just trying to get us in the mood for a werewolf hunt."

"Please don't do that again," Liza said. "This place is creepy enough without your special effects."

"Well, if we're going, let's get it over with," Melody said.

"All right," Howie said, "Mr. Youngblood is staying in Dr. Herb's old house at the edge of the cemetery."

"How do you know that?" Eddie asked.

Howie tapped his forehead. "I read the newspaper. It's amazing the things you can learn from reading."

Liza took a deep breath and crossed Green Street. Her three friends followed her when she turned left onto Olympus Lane. There was plenty of light from the full moon so Melody switched off her flashlight. The minute they stepped onto Olympus Lane, three dogs barked. "Shh," Liza warned her friends, "or they'll hear us coming."

"We could march a band down the middle of the street and they couldn't hear us over the racket those dogs are making," Eddie said, but he kept quiet after that.

Olympus Lane had only a few houses on it, and every house was like a palace. Some of the homes even had gates that required a combination to open them. Howie stopped in front of a huge three-story house that had at least ten columns holding up the porch roof.

"Whoever lives here now must be a millionaire," Eddie said. "I wonder if they'd mind sharing a few bucks with me."

"My mom said that the lady who lives here gave Mr. Youngblood money to pay for his television ads and stuff," Melody said.

"Maybe I'll run for president and get donations," Eddie said, rubbing his hands together.

Liza rolled her eyes at Eddie. "I'm pretty sure you can't spend the money on toys or candy."

"Then what's the point?" Eddie asked.

"Shh," Howie said. "We need to concentrate on sneaking up to the house."

Eddie immediately went into spy mode. He sank down low to the ground and tiptoed beside a big clump of bushes. He was so busy acting like a spy that he

didn't see a big hand coming out of the bushes.

"Gotcha!" a voice yelled. A security agent pulled Eddie up by his collar.

"Let me go!" Eddie screamed.

"You kids again," the agent said, shaking her head. "What are you doing here?"

Liza's face went red. "Um . . . we wanted to see Mr. Youngblood one more time," she stammered.

"Oh, you'll see him all right," the agent said. "Come with me." The kids followed the agent, who still had Eddie by the collar.

The agent opened the huge door to the mansion. The kids couldn't believe what they saw.

7

Weredog

"This is worse than a horror movie," Eddie groaned.

Cobwebs filled the dark hallway inside the house. A big couch stood on one side, but most of the stuffing had been torn out. Deep scratches covered the walls and the staircase. The smell of wet fur hung in the air. Dog toys and half-chewed bones littered the floor.

The agent let Eddie go. "Follow me," she ordered the kids.

"Whatever belongs to those chew toys got carried away. I wonder what kind of dog it is," Melody said.

"I know," Liza whimpered. "It's a were-dog."

"Shh," Howie warned as the security agent led them deeper into the house.

43

The kids stared at the walls as they followed the agent. Campaign posters were plastered everywhere.

"Is this guy loco?" Eddie wanted to know. "He can't seriously believe people will vote for those things."

"Excuse me," Melody asked the agent. "What do you think Mr. Youngblood will do to us?"

The agent turned to glare at Melody. "Well, you were trespassing on private property. What do *you* think he'll do?"

Melody gulped and Eddie whispered in

her ear. "Mr. Youngblood will probably eat us for a midnight snack."

Liza gasped and pointed to another poster. "TAKE THE JUNK OUT OF SCHOOL LUNCHES," she read.

"Oh, great," Eddie said. "First this nut wants to make us go to school every day of the year from dawn to dusk, now he wants to take away French fries, pizza, and potato chips."

"Who's going to vote for that?" Melody asked.

"I'll tell you who," a low voice growled from behind them. The kids turned around and came face-to-face with Mr. Youngblood himself. He was even hairier than they remembered and now he wore a torn T-shirt and dirty blue jeans.

"Your parents!" he said. "That's who!" And then Mr. Youngblood howled with laughter.

8

A Howling Good Plan

An entire week had passed and Mr. Youngblood hadn't left Bailey City as he'd originally planned. Now the kids stood amid a huge crowd gathered in front of the Bailey City Library. The presidential candidate stood on the top step, making another speech.

"This is terrible," Eddie moaned.

"It's not terrible," Howie said. "It's great that so many people in Bailey City are paying attention to politics. After all, that's what democracy is all about."

"I'm glad Mr. Youngblood didn't call the police on us last week," Melody admitted. Mr. Youngblood had spent nearly thirty minutes asking the kids about what they did in school before he had security agents walk them home.

"The police wouldn't have asked so many questions," Eddie complained as a nearby lady asked him to be quiet.

Stone gargoyles peered down from the library roof, but they didn't seem half as scary as Mr. Youngblood. The cold autumn wind whipped his hair into tangles, and red circles rimmed his eyes. Liza shivered, and it wasn't just from the wind. She didn't like the way the candidate's eyes flashed over the crowd as if he were looking for his next meal.

The rest of the people gathered in front of the library didn't notice. As Mr. Youngblood's voice rose and fell, the crowd broke into applause.

"Look," Howie said. "There's Mr. Jenkins and Harry Goto."

"Who's that with them?" Melody asked.

A pack of people stood close to the candidate. Every one of them had long snarled hair. Only these people didn't look like they ever tried to comb out tangles.

"They must be supporters," Howie said with a nod.

Most of the people in the crowd supported Mr. Youngblood for president. Only a few people toward the back disagreed with him. Ranger Lily held a sign that read VOTE YES FOR THE ENVIRONMENT BY VOTING NO FOR YOUNGBLOOD.

Mr. Youngblood didn't talk about the environment. He pounded on a podium and bellowed over the voices of the crowd. "We must focus our energy on the most important issue facing our nation," he said. "And that's education!"

Most of the adults applauded. Eddie sighed. His grandmother stood at the front of the crowd staring up at Mr. Youngblood. Eddie knew for a fact that his grandmother believed reading, writing, and arithmetic were better than video games and soccer any day.

Mr. Youngblood continued, his voice growing louder until he was yelling. "I'm talking about making our schools the best in the entire world. My plan will work. I don't just say it's good. I say it's THE HOWLING BEST!"

With that, Mr. Youngblood lifted his face to the sky and let out a blood-curdling howl. He wasn't the only one. Mr. Jenkins and the whole group of hairy supporters joined in with wolf calls of their own.

The crowd broke out in another round of applause. At least, the adults did. The kids weren't too sure what to do.

"Why does he keep talking about school?" Eddie muttered. "Why does he keep talking at all? Someone needs to stop him."

"You can't stop him," Liza pointed out. "The Bill of Rights guarantees his right of free speech."

Mr. Youngblood yelled, "I ask you, how are our children spending their weekends? I'll tell you how. They're wasting the days away when they could be *learning*! When I'm elected, schools will be

open on Saturdays so learning can continue uninterrupted. We'll have longer school days and healthier lunches. We will be the world leaders in education!"

The adults in the crowd cheered again, but not Melody, Liza, Howie, and Eddie.

"I can't believe people are buying this," Eddie said.

"I can't believe a werewolf might be the next president of the United States," Liza muttered under her breath.

Mr. Youngblood's eyes flashed over the crowd. The wind whipped back his hair. He raised a hairy hand in the air, silencing the crowd. "The truth is, I can't wait until I'm elected. I want to start pushing for longer school days RIGHT NOW! RIGHT HERE! IN BAILEY CITY!"

"What?" Melody gasped as the crowd cheered.

"What is he talking about?" Eddie asked. "He can't do that, can he?"

"Shh," Howie said, "and we'll find out."

Mr. Youngblood pounded the podium

with his hairy fist. "I've met with the principal and held meetings with the mayor of your fine town. I've talked with a group of students."

Melody gulped. "I think he means us!"

Mr. Youngblood's voice bellowed out his next words. "I'm here to tell you that tomorrow Bailey Elementary will become the first school to put my plan into action."

"What plan?" Eddie gasped.

Eddie's face grew pale. Then he turned a sickly shade of green as Mr. Youngblood ticked off his plan on his hairy fingers.

9

Werewolf Battle

"Shorter recesses. Longer days. Healthy food. What kind of plan is that?" Eddie groaned when he met up with Melody, Liza, and Howie the next morning. "This is going to be the worst day of my life!"

The four kids sighed as they made their way through the mob of people on the Bailey School playground. Mr. Youngblood was surrounded by Mr. Jenkins and a pack of hairy supporters. Television and newspaper reporters pushed toward the candidate, their cameras whirring. A reporter from the WMTJ television station fixed her makeup on the steps leading into the building. The nearby television van's antenna reached high into the sky.

"Today is the day that Mr. Youngblood

puts his education plan to the test," the reporter told the camera as soon as the red light on the camera blinked to life. "It may, indeed, be his first action as the newest president of the United States."

"He's not even president yet," Howie gasped. "He hasn't been elected. How can this be happening?"

"It's our parents' fault," Melody said. "I asked my mom last night and she said everyone thinks kids need to learn, learn, learn. Parents are the ones voting, and Mr. Youngblood knows it. He'll say whatever it takes to get elected."

"And once he's in office," Liza said, "we'd better be-WARE. As in WERE-wolf!"

"Work, work, work. That's the secret of success," Mr. Youngblood told the WMTJ reporter. "And that's what I plan for the students of Bailey City — to make them hard workers, just like me!"

Mr. Youngblood was right. Working was exactly what the kids did. As soon as

they sat at their desks, their teacher put them right to work.

Things weren't *too* bad until lunch. That's when the kids of Bailey City got a taste of Mr. Youngblood's healthy food.

"What is this mush?" Eddie asked when the cafeteria lady slapped a mound of brown goop on his tray.

Melody sniffed the steaming mound of mush. "It smells familiar," she said. "I just can't place it."

Howie bent over his tray and took a big whiff. "I know," he said, his face draining of color. "It smells like dog food!"

"Of course it does," Liza said. "That's because it *is* dog food. What else would a werewolf eat — besides helpless kids?"

By the end of the day, the kids were exhausted. Already, the sun was fading in the sky when the bell finally rang. Their backpacks were heavy with books and homework. Most kids dragged themselves home without a second glance at the playground.

Not Eddie. He pulled his friends to the deep shadows of the oak tree. "Mr. Youngblood has gone too far," he said.

"I agree," Liza said.

"You do?" Eddie asked. He wasn't used to Liza agreeing with him.

Liza nodded. "Mr. Youngblood *cannot* be elected president. He plans to turn our schools into werewolf training grounds."

"What are you talking about?" Melody asked.

Liza explained it all. "Mr. Youngblood has taken over our school and he's feeding us dog food. He makes us stay in school until the moon is peeping up over the horizon. He even said he wants to make us just like him. It's as simple as one, two, three. Mr. Youngblood is planning on turning us into werewolves like Mr. Jenkins and the rest of his hairy supporters. Soon, everyone in Bailey School will be howling at the moon!"

Howie, Melody, and Eddie looked at Liza for a full thirteen seconds. Liza

expected them to laugh at her idea, but they didn't.

"What are we going to do?" Howie finally asked.

Liza looked around the playground to make sure no one was listening. The other kids were so exhausted they didn't bother looking around. They just dragged their tired bodies home. "I thought about it until the moon was high in the sky last night," she told them. "There's only one way we can win this werewolf battle. We have to do exactly what Mrs. Jeepers wants us to do."

The kids looked at Liza with strange expressions on their faces. After all, they thought their teacher was a vampire.

"You mean," Melody finally squeaked, "we're going to suck blood?"

10

Kids' Campaign

"Mrs. Jeepers taught us about free speech," Liza explained to her friends as they sat around her kitchen table.

Eddie took a sip of milk to wash down his chocolate chip cookie. "Mr. Youngblood's free speech is what's gotten us into this mess," Eddie grumbled, with milk dribbling down his chin. Howie and Melody nodded.

"What can we do?" Howie asked. "The election is only a few days away and Mr. Youngblood has the voters convinced his ideas are the best."

"Then we have to show them that he's wrong," Liza said with a firm voice.

"How do we do that?" Eddie asked.

"By organizing our own campaign," Liza said with her eyes shining.

"I get it," Melody said, jumping up from her seat. "We can protest, just like Ranger Lily and her friends were doing."

And that's exactly what the kids did. They got on the phone and called everyone they knew, even the school bully. Pretty soon, every kid in Bailey City was making posters.

The next afternoon a hundred kids met on the steps of the library after another long day at school and started chanting.

"Vote no to Mr. Youngblood!"

"Let kids be kids!"

The kids raised their signs up and marched around the library columns. Parents walked by and shook their heads, but the next day nothing changed at school. The bell rang early and the teachers put them to work. Brown mush was plopped on their lunch trays and the sun was setting by the time their teachers gave them a long list of homework.

"What are we going to do?" Melody asked. The four kids were drinking apple

cider at Liza's house, trying to recover from a hard day of work, work, work.

"We've got the kids behind us," Liza said. "Now we have to take our campaign to the people who can make a difference. The voters! We have to show our parents what voting for Mr. Youngblood will REALLY mean."

"But we carried our signs," Melody told her. "We marched and chanted. It's not our fault if the voters didn't pay attention."

"Then we have to make them hear us," Liza said. "And we have to do it now. The election is on Tuesday. We can't waste a single minute."

The kids gulped the rest of their cider, threw on their coats, and headed for the skating rink.

"Do you realize that kids will no longer have time to skate?" Liza asked Frank, the rink manager. "We'll be much too busy with school stuff."

Melody nodded. "I bet they'll have to

close down the rink because it's not being used."

Next, they went to the ice cream and candy stores. "We probably won't be here to spend our allowances," Eddie told the owners. "We'll only be eating Mr. Youngblood's healthy foods from now on."

The kids found Miky Yo in the Bonsai Bakery putting icing on a wedding cake. "We love your bakery," Howie told him. "But since Mr. Youngblood only wants us to eat mush, our parents probably won't let us come here to buy cookies anymore."

The kids visited business after business. They even stopped Mr. Jenkins when they saw him leaving the pet store with a huge bag of dog food slung over his shoulder. "If Mr. Youngblood wins the election," Liza said, "we won't be coming to Camp Lone Wolf anymore.

"Our summer vacations will be spent researching," Eddie told him.

"We'll be working, working, working," Melody added.

Mr. Jenkins let the bag of dog food slip to the ground. He scratched his chin and thought about what the kids had said.

"Going from person to person is taking way too much time," Liza moaned as they hurried around a corner and plopped on a step to rest. "We'll never get to all the voters in time."

"You're right," Eddie said. "There's only one thing left for us to do."

11

Eddie's Press Conference

"Good evening, ladies and gentlemen of the press," Howie told the reporters who stood on the steps of the library the next day. Not only local reporters were crowded at the base of the steps, but national reporters took notes as well. Howie had arranged the whole thing using the Internet. "Thank you for coming to our press conference. We are here to address the issue of Mr. Youngblood's educational program."

Melody stepped up to the microphone as photographers flashed her picture, and bright lights from TV cameras glared in her eyes. "We agree that education is very important," Melody said clearly.

Liza nodded. "But we disagree with Mr. Youngblood's methods. We decided not to vote for him in our school election and we hope you won't vote for him in the national election, either."

"What's this?" Mr. Youngblood roared from the rear of the crowd. "Somebody get these kids out of here!"

A couple of security agents in dark suits moved toward the kids, and Liza grabbed Melody's arm. Liza's voice squeaked as she spoke into the microphone. "Our teacher said our country is founded on the idea of free speech, and that's why we're here."

"The kids have the right to speak," the reporter from WMTJ shouted.

"Let them talk," Ranger Lily yelled from the side.

The security agents stopped when Mr. Cooper, the librarian, blocked them. A huge crowd of voters gathered as Eddie moved in front of the microphone.

"We only have one chance to be kids," he said. "Is it fair to make us give up sports and playing with friends? You

adults must remember what it was like to be young. Don't we deserve the right to play?"

A quiet came over the crowd as Liza patted Eddie on the back. In fact, only one sound echoed from the rear of the mob.

"No!!!!!" Mr. Youngblood howled.

But he was too late. The crowd gasped. Cameras whirred. Howie's, Melody's, Liza's, and Eddie's words were heard loud and clear across the entire nation.

"I can't watch," Liza said a few days later, hiding her eyes behind her hands. The kids sat in Melody's family room with the election news blaring on the TV. Their parents had given them permission to stay up extra late to see the election results. "Did he win? Is Mr. Youngblood our next president?"

Reporters read results from voting booths across the country. Maps showing which candidate had the most votes flashed across the screen. Finally, Eddie jumped up from the couch and danced around. "He lost! Mr. Youngblood lost!" Eddie sang.

Liza opened her eyes as the screen flashed the words YOUNGBLOOD DEFEATED!

"We did it!" Liza cheered.

Eddie flopped down on the couch. "This democracy business is harder than doing book reports," he said.

"We really do have the power to make a difference," Howie said, "even though we're just kids. We were a political machine."

Melody smiled. "That's right," she said. "Maybe we should think of other things that need changing."

"I know what we should change," Eddie said, jumping off the couch to stand in the middle of the floor. "First, no homework. Then, no chores. Next, no . . ."

Eddie continued his list while Melody rolled her eyes and pointed to Eddie. "That's not a political machine. That's a political monster!"

Liza giggled. "It seems like there's always room for another monster in Bailey City!"

Election
Facts

Did you know . . .

1. In a **democracy**, citizens have the right to elect the people who will represent them in the government. The United States of America is a democracy.

2. The Bill of Rights lists **freedoms** Americans have as citizens of the United States of America.

3. Just as Liza said, **the Bill of Rights** gives people freedom of speech and the right to assemble.

4. Women weren't allowed to vote until the 19th Amendment was passed in August of 1920. It took 42 years after the bill was first introduced in 1878 before Congress passed it. During those 42 years, people worked hard to get the amendment passed. These people were called **suffragists**. They marched, carried banners, and gave speeches just like the people in *Werewolves Don't Run For President* do.

5. Women weren't the first group of people to fight for **the right to vote**. African American males weren't al-lowed to vote until 1870 and Native Americans weren't allowed to vote until 1924.

6. A **political party** is a group of people who have ideas in common and who work to get its members elected. In America, there are two main political parties.

7. The symbol for the **Republican party** is the elephant. It was first used in the 19th century in a cartoon by Thomas Nast.

8. The symbol for the **Democratic party** is a donkey. It was first used by Andrew Jackson in 1828 to represent his stubbornness.

9. A **campaign trail** describes the

series of places where a candidate goes to make speeches and get support.

10. All candidates have **platforms**, which describe what they believe in. People usually vote for the candidate whose platform they agree with most.

11. George Washington was the first President of the United States. So far, there have been **43 presidents** of the United States. (As far as we know, none were werewolves.)

☆ Presidential Fast Facts ☆

1. Nine presidents didn't go to college.

2. Andrew Johnson, our 17th president, couldn't read until he was 14.

3. William Howard Taft was our biggest president. He weighed more than 300 pounds!

4. You have to be 35 years old to be president. Ronald Reagan was 69 when he first ran for pres-

ident. The youngest
elected president was
John F. Kennedy. He
was just 43 years old
when he became
president.

5. Eight presidents
were born in log cabins.

6. Abraham Lincoln was
the tallest president. He
was six feet four
inches tall.

7. James Madison
was the shortest president.
He was five feet four
inches tall.

8. Six presidents were
named James:
  • James Madison
  • James Monroe
  • James Polk
  • James Buchanan
  • James Garfield
  • James (Jimmy) Carter

About the Authors

Debbie Dadey and Marcia Thornton Jones have fun writing stories together. When they both worked at an elementary school in Lexington, Kentucky, Debbie was the school librarian and Marcia was a teacher. During their lunch break in the school cafeteria, they came up with the idea of the Bailey School Kids.

Debbie and her family live in Fort Collins, Colorado. Marcia and her husband still live in Kentucky.

You can learn more about Debbie and Marcia on their Web pages: http://www.debbiedadey.com and http://www.marciatjones.com.

About the Illustrator

John Steven Gurney has illustrated more than 100 books for children including the Bailey School Kids, the Bailey City Monsters, and the Big Apple Barn series. His illustrations have appeared in magazines, *TV Guide*, and even the board game Guess Who?. He lives in Brattleboro, Vermont with his wife and their two children.

You can learn more about him on his Web site: http://www.johnstevengurney.com.

Some of your favorite Adventures of

The BAILEY SCHOOL KIDS

have a brand-new look!

Check out all of them!

Don't miss these

The

BAILEY SCHOOL KIDS

Special Editions!

Super Special #1: Mrs. Jeepers Is Missing!

Super Special #2: Mrs. Jeepers' Batty Vacation

Super Special #3: Mrs. Jeepers' Secret Cave

Super Special #4: Mrs. Jeepers in Outer Space

Super Special #5: Mrs. Jeepers' Monster Class Trip

Super Special #6: Mrs. Jeepers on Vampire Island

Super Special #7: Mrs. Jeepers' Scariest Halloween Ever

Each book has pages of MONSTER-ously
fun puzzles and activities inside!

**Other series by Debbie Dadey
and Marcia Thornton Jones**

Ghostville Elementary

Other books by Debbie Dadey

The Slime Wars

Slime Time

The Swamp Monster in Third Grade series

The Worst Name in Third Grade

Other books by Marcia Thornton Jones

Champ

Godzilla Ate My Homework

Jack Frost